C000148209

**Faber
Stories**

Adrian Tomine

Intruders

Faber Stories

ff

First published in this edition in 2019
by Faber & Faber Limited
Bloomsbury House
74–77 Great Russell Street
London WC1B 3DA
First published in *Killing and Dying* in 2015

Typeset by Faber & Faber Limited
Printed and bound by CPI Group (UK) Ltd, Croydon, CR0 4YY

A CIP record for this book
is available from the British Library

ISBN 978–0–571–35597–6

10 9 8 7 6 5 4 3 2 1

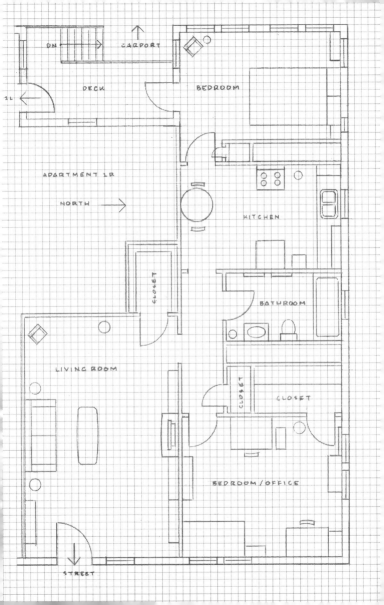

for Yoshihiro Tatsumi

BETWEEN MY SECOND
AND THIRD TOURS, I
CAME BACK TO A
BUNCH OF BULLSHIT
AND NOT MUCH ELSE.

I HAD A COUSIN WHO
LET ME CRASH IN
HER BASEMENT. SHE
WAS MARRIED WITH
THREE KIDS.

ONE NIGHT I HEARD
THEM ALL TALKING
ABOUT ME THROUGH
THE CEILING, AND
SOME OF THE THINGS
THEY SAID JUST
ABOUT KILLED ME.

I ENDED UP AT A
PLACE CALLED
EXTENDED STAY
AMERICA, OUT BY THE
CAR DEALERSHIPS
AND STRIP MALLS.

RIGHT ACROSS THE
FREEWAY WAS AN
IN-N-OUT, A KRISPY
KREME, AND A PANDA
EXPRESS.

I FIGURED WORSE
CAME TO WORSE, I
COULD ALWAYS EAT
MYSELF TO DEATH AND
THE AUTOPSY WOULD
STILL COME BACK
CLEAN.

ONE OF THOSE PLACES, THAT'S WHERE I RAN INTO THE GIRL, WHAT-EVER HER NAME WAS.

I BLUFFED MY WAY
THROUGH ABOUT TEN
MINUTES OF SMALL
TALK BEFORE IT
FINALLY CLICKED.

SHE WAS SOMEONE'S KID OR NIECE OR SOME-THING. SHE HOUSE-SAT FOR ME AND MARIA THAT TIME WE WENT TO CATALINA.

I DIDN'T LIKE THE IDEA OF SOMEONE STAYING THERE, BUT MARIA HAD A THING ABOUT LEAVING THE APARTMENT EMPTY.

I WAS SUPPOSED TO
GO PICK UP THE KEYS
FROM THE GIRL WHEN
WE GOT BACK, BUT I
KEPT PUTTING IT OFF.

THEN SHE OFFERED TO DROP THEM BY SOMETIME, AND THEN MARIA WAS GONNA GET THEM, BUT EVENTUALLY WE ALL JUST FORGOT ABOUT IT.

THEY WERE JUST
COPIES, ANYWAY,
MADE AT THE HARD-
WARE STORE FOR A
BUCK A PIECE.

STANDING THERE IN THE PARKING LOT, I SHOULD'VE JUST BACKTRACKED AND EXPLAINED EVERY-THING, BUT THE RIGHT MOMENT NEVER CAME.

I GUESS I GOT SWEPT UP IN HER EXCITE-MENT AND DIDN'T WANT TO MAKE THINGS AWKWARD.

17

BACK AT THE HOTEL,
I STARED AT THE KEYS
FOR AWHILE, THREW
THEM IN THE TRASH,
AND WENT TO SLEEP.

NEXT MORNING, I WOKE UP, DUG THE KEYS OUT OF THE TRASH, AND CAUGHT A BUS INTO TOWN.

THE CAFE ACROSS
FROM OUR APART-
MENT DIDN'T SELL
COFFEE ANYMORE,
THANKS TO THE NEW
PEET'S UP THE BLOCK.

NOW THEY SPECIAL-
IZED IN CREPES,
SMOOTHIES, AND
SOME SHIT CALLED
BUBBLE TEA.

I WAS DYING FOR
A COFFEE, BUT THE
TRUTH IS, I WAS JUST
THERE FOR THE VIEW.

IT WAS DEPRESSING
TO SEE EVERYONE
TRAPPED ON THE
SAME HAMSTER
WHEEL. GO TO WORK,
COME HOME, REPEAT.

I TRACKED THE GUY
IN OUR OLD PLACE
FOR A WEEK, AND THE
ONLY THING THAT
CHANGED WAS THE
COLOR OF HIS SUIT.

NO ONE REALLY GIVES A SHIT ABOUT RENT-ERS, BUT A DECENT LANDLORD WILL RE-KEY THE LOCKS AS A BASIC SECURITY MEASURE WHEN A PLACE TURNS OVER.

THE OLD CHINESE
GUY WOULD'VE DONE
IT. EVERYTHING
WENT DOWNHILL
WHEN HE CROAKED
AND HIS SCUMBAG
KIDS TOOK OVER.

WE HAD TO MAIL OUR
KEYS TO THE DAUGH-
TER TO GET OUR DE-
POSIT BACK WHEN WE
LEFT, BUT SO WHAT?

IT SMELLED DIFFER-
ENT. THAT'S WHAT I
NOTICED BEFORE
ANYTHING ELSE.

ONCE I MADE SURE
THE PLACE WAS
EMPTY, I OPENED A
FEW WINDOWS TO
AIR IT OUT.

EVERYTHING WAS UP-
GRADED, REPAIRED,
RE-DONE. MARIA
WOULD'VE LOVED IT.

THINGS THAT WE
LEARNED TO LIVE
WITH, LIKE THE
PEELING PAINT IN
THE BATHROOM AND
THE BROKEN LIGHT
IN THE FRIDGE, HAD
ALL BEEN TAKEN
CARE OF.

BUT THERE WAS ENOUGH THAT HADN'T CHANGED: SAME FIXTURES, SAME APPLIANCES, SAME SHIT-BROWN CARPET IN THE BEDROOM.

I FOUND THE HOLE
IN THE WALL THAT
I'D PUNCHED AND
THEN PUTTIED OVER.
THE BATHROOM
SHELF I PUT UP WAS
STILL THERE.

THE GUY EVEN KEPT
THE COBWEBBY
PIECE OF 2X4 I
USED TO PROP THE
KITCHEN WINDOW
OPEN.

I COULD'VE SNOOPED AROUND, TURNED ON THE COMPUTER, RIFLED THROUGH THE DRAWERS, BUT THAT'S A LINE I WOULDN'T CROSS.

THERE'S A MILLION
THINGS I COULD'VE
DONE, BUT I'D SATIS-
FIED MY CURIOSITY
AND THAT WAS THAT.

I COULDN'T SLEEP
THAT NIGHT, AND
THE SAME STUPID
THOUGHT KEPT RAT-
TLING AROUND IN
MY HEAD: THAT THE
GUY WOULD COME
HOME AND NOTICE THE
MISSING EGG.

OF COURSE THE
PROBABILITY OF
THAT WAS SLIM, AND
PLUS, WHAT WAS HE
GONNA DO? CALL THE
COPS TO REPORT IT?

BUT I'D BEEN CARE-
LESS AND IT NAGGED
AT ME. I COULDN'T DO
ANYTHING ABOUT IT
UNTIL MORNING, AND
THAT MADE IT EVEN
WORSE.

THE KID AT SAFEWAY
WOULDN'T JUST SELL
ME AN EGG, SO I
BOUGHT A DOZEN.

I PUT ONE IN MY POCKET, TOSSED THE REST, AND —— WHEN THE COAST WAS CLEAR —— WENT BACK TO THE APARTMENT.

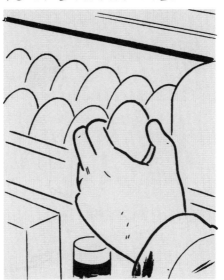

IT FELT GOOD TO
SOLVE A PROBLEM,
TO MAKE SOMETHING
RIGHT, NO MATTER
HOW SMALL.

AFTER THAT, I GUESS
I FELL INTO A ROU-
TINE JUST LIKE
EVERYONE ELSE.

THE GUY AT THE
BUBBLE TEA PLACE
STARTED MAKING
COFFEE AGAIN, JUST
FOR ME.

SOME DAYS I'D BRING
A LUNCH WITH ME,
ALWAYS MAKING
SURE TO CLEAN UP
AND REMOVE ANY
TRASH.

I SET THE ALARM ON
MY WATCH TO AVOID
ANY OVERLAP.

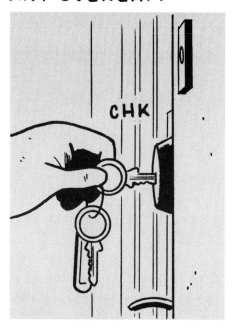

I SKETCHED A FLOOR-
PLAN AND WORKED
OUT SOME EXIT
STRATEGIES, JUST
IN CASE.

BUT FOR THE MOST
PART, IT'S HARD TO
SAY HOW I PASSED
THOSE HOURS, TO
BE HONEST.

THAT ONE DAY, I'D
ACTUALLY FALLEN
ASLEEP WHEN IT
ALL STARTED.

I ALMOST ANSWERED
THE DOOR OUT OF
HABIT.

IT WAS A KID, PROB-
ABLY HIGH SCHOOL
AGE. I FIGURED HE
WAS LOOKING FOR A
DONATION OR A
SIGNATURE ON A
PETITION.

HE RANG THE DOOR-
BELL A FEW TIMES,
THEN KNOCKED
AGAIN BEFORE
GIVING UP.

A FEW MINUTES
LATER, I HEARD THE
SCREEN FROM THE
BATHROOM WINDOW
CLATTERING INTO
THE BATHTUB.

BY THE TIME I GOT
THERE, THE KID WAS
HALFWAY THROUGH
THE WINDOW.

I REACTED ON PURE
INSTINCT, LIKE IT
WAS STILL MY HOME
TO PROTECT.

IT FELT LIKE THE POWER COMING BACK ON AFTER A BLACKOUT.

I WAS A HUNDRED
PERCENT IN THE
RIGHT. WHATEVER
HAPPENED, THE KID
HAD IT COMING.

HE WAS SLOPPY AND
SCARED, BUT HE
MANAGED TO THINK
ON HIS FEET.

IT WAS A GIFT--LIKE
HE'D JUST GIVEN ME
PERMISSION TO TURN
IT UP A NOTCH.

STILL, I HELD BACK.
THE LAST THING I
NEEDED WAS AN
AMBULANCE SHOW-
ING UP THERE.

THE KID HAD ME OVER A BARREL AND HE DIDN'T EVEN KNOW IT.

I WALKED DOWN THE
HALL AND OPENED
THE BACK DOOR. COOL
AIR BLEW IN FROM
THE ALLEY.

I DON'T KNOW WHAT I WAS EXPECTING, EXACTLY. DID HE UNDERSTAND HOW LUCKY HE WAS?

AFTER THAT IT WAS
A RACE AGAINST THE
CLOCK TO GET EVERY-
THING BACK IN
ORDER.

IT TOOK LONGER
THAN I EXPECTED,
AND ALL I WANTED TO
DO WAS GET OUT.

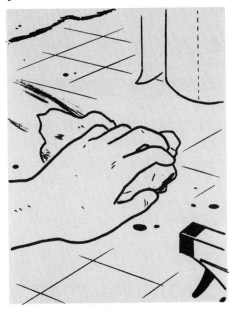

I WAS JUST ABOUT
DONE WHEN I REAL-
IZED I'D DEPLETED
THE GUY'S CLEANING
SUPPLIES.

IT WAS A LONG
AFTERNOON.

THE LAST DAY, I WAS
LATER THAN USUAL.

I CAN'T REMEMBER
HOW IT STARTED,
BUT I GOT INTO A
LITTLE SQUABBLE
WITH THE GUY AT
THE CAFE.

HE MADE A COMMENT--
A LITTLE PASSIVE-
AGRESSIVE DIG--AND
AFTER ALL THE
MONEY I'D PUT IN
HIS COFFERS, IT
BOTHERED ME.

THE LIGHTS WERE ON
IN THE APARTMENT
WHEN I GOT THERE.
THAT SHOULD'VE
TIPPED ME OFF.

AS I MOVED TOWARD
THE KITCHEN, I
HEARD A SERIES OF
SOUNDS: A THUD,
SOMETHING CLAT-
TERING ACROSS THE
FLOOR, A MOAN.

SHE MUST'VE BEEN AT LEAST EIGHTY, MAYBE OLDER. WAS SHE THE GUY'S MOTHER? HIS GRANDMOTHER?

SHE STARTED
SCREAMING IN
SOME LANGUAGE I
DIDN'T KNOW, AND
SHE WOULDN'T STOP.

I TRIED TO HELP HER
UP AND MAKE SURE
SHE WASN'T HURT,
BUT SHE KICKED AND
SPAT AT ME AND
SHRIEKED EVEN
LOUDER.

I WANTED TO APOLO-
GIZE AND EXPLAIN
EVERYTHING, BUT
MOST OF ALL I WANT-
ED TO DISAPPEAR.

I LOCKED THE DOOR
BEHIND ME WHEN I
LEFT. I LISTENED
FOR SIRENS, ALMOST
HOPING THAT I'D
HEAR THEM.

I WALKED UP THE
BLOCK, INTO THE
STREAM OF OBLIV-
IOUS, HAPPY
PEOPLE WITH THEIR
FAMILIES, THEIR
SHOPPING, THEIR
CHATTER.

AND STARTING RIGHT THERE, I TRIED MY BEST TO BECOME ONE OF THEM.